W9-ART-202

To my lifelong friend Linda Smith,
who was never scared stiff

www.harcourt.com

Library of Congress Cataloging-in-Publication Data
Davis, Katie.
Scared stiff/Katie Davis.
p.   cm.
Summary: A little girl devises a clever way to face her fears and discovers that she really doesn't have anything to be afraid of.
[1. Fear-Fiction.]   I. Title.
PZ7.D2944Sc   2001
[E]–dc21   00-8473
ISBN 0-15-202305-4

First edition
A C E G H F D B

Printed in Singapore

The illustrations in this book were done in acrylic paints and pen on hot press Arches watercolor paper.
The display type and text type were set in Heatwave.
Color separations by Bright Arts Ltd., Hong Kong
Printed and bound by Tien Wah Press, Singapore
This book was printed on totally chlorine-free Nymolla Matte Art paper.
Production supervision by Sandra Grebenar and Ginger Boyer
Designed by Linda Lockowitz

Scared Stiff

Written and illustrated by

KATIE DAVIS

HARCOURT, INC. San Diego New York London

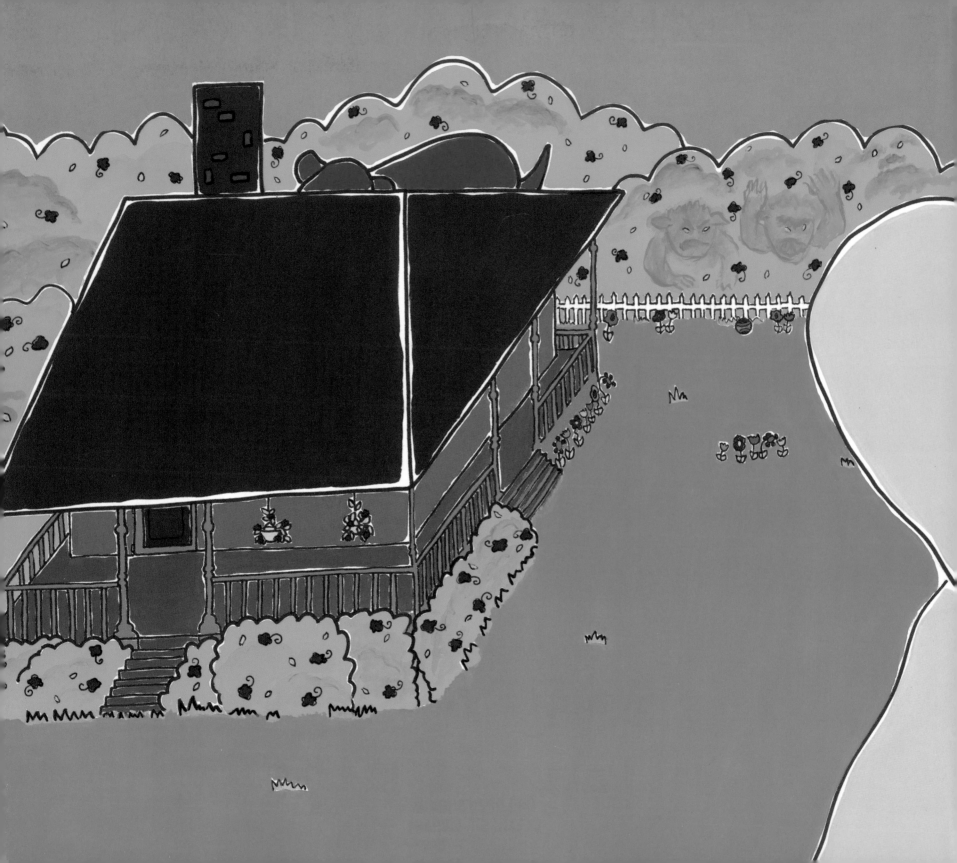

I am scared stiff.

To begin with, there's Ono. That's not his real name.
I call him that because every time I see him I say,

That dog loves children...

...for lunch.

But I run so fast that by the time he sees me...

...I'm already gone.

Ono is bad.
But the monsters are way worse.

So I use my Monster Diversion Technique.

Everyone knows monsters love gross stuff,
so I sing a slimy eyeball song to keep them happy.

It's a short song, so it's a good thing I'm a fast runner.

Then there are the snakes that live in my closet.
I can see them peeking out under the door…

…so I never open it.

This is NOT a good way to live.

So I've decided to turn into a witch,

because witches aren't afraid of anything.

I cackled.

Nothing happened.

I held my breath until I turned blue.
Then I remembered witches are actually green.

I put on really long fake fingernails. But they fell off.

I was running out of ideas when all of a sudden
I remembered the magic words!

It must've worked, because I felt different.

But something still wasn't right.

Much better.

Now it was safe to go outside and play. But I needed my jacket.

And my jacket was in the closet.

"Oh yeah!" I remembered. "I'm a fearless witch!"
I yanked open my closet door.

I couldn't believe what I saw....

A bazillion tangled-up shoelaces? No slithery snakes?

I've been scared stiff of SHOELACES?!
I grabbed my coat and went out to play.

There was only one little problem.

My ball was right in front of the bushes where the monsters live.
There was a huge claw sticking out and then I saw...

...leaves and sticks and stuff? No monsters?

I've been scared stiff of a SHRUB?!

My stomach started growling,
so I ate an old piece of candy I found in my pocket.
But the growling didn't stop.

In fact, it was getting louder. I felt like dinner....

Ono's dinner.

But the growling wasn't Ono.
And it wasn't even my stomach.

It was...

...six hungry puppies? Ono was a mom?

All this time I've been scared stiff of PUPPIES?!

I walked away from Ono and her babies—verrry slowly.

I didn't want to scare them.

I skipped past the bush, and bounced my ball,

and sang my slimy eyeball song for old times' sake.

I went inside and opened my closet door to hang up my jacket.

"Hello, you slithery shoelaces," I said.

Maybe I didn't need to be a witch.

After all, there was nothing to be afraid of anymore.

But just in case...

...I think I'll save this.

For emergencies.